The Mermaid of Zennor

by Lynne Benton and Daniel Duncan

FRANKLIN WATTS
LONDON•SYDNEY

About this story

Zennor is a tiny village perched high above rocky Penwith Cove in West
Cornwall. In the church of St Senara (old Cornish for Zennor) you can see
"the mermaid chair" with its carving of the mermaid holding a comb and
a mirror. Nobody knows whether the carving or the story came first,
but it is now a well-known Cornish legend.

The Mermaid of Zennor

Contents

Chapter 1

The Church

The heavy oak door creaked open. The church seemed
gloomy after the bright summer sunshine, and smelled
musty. The pews were made of dark wood, heavily carved,
and it all looked very old. Ella shivered as she felt
a sudden chill in the air.

She hoped Dad wouldn't be too long. He was outside,
answering his phone, but he'd told her to go into
the church and look for a very unusual carving.

Ella began looking around her. She wished she knew
exactly what she was trying to find.

"Are you looking for something, my dear?"
asked a gentle voice out of the gloom.

Ella jumped.

She'd thought the church was empty, but now she could
see that there was an old woman sitting in one of
the pews. She had a lace cap on her head and a blue shawl
round her shoulders, and she looked strangely
old-fashioned. Her voice, however, was kind.

"I'm sorry, I didn't see you there," said Ella. "My dad told
me I'd find an interesting carving in here, but I don't know
where it is."

The old woman smiled. "He was right, my dear," she said.
"But you cannot see it from there. If you come over here,
I can show you."

Ella hesitated. She'd been told not to talk to strangers but Dad was just outside, so surely it couldn't hurt to go a bit closer, could it? She was curious to see the carving. Cautiously, she walked towards the pew. Although the old woman's face was pale and wrinkled, her eyes were bright blue. Ella felt as though they could see right through her. She shivered. Then she noticed that the woman was wearing a beautiful necklace made of tiny seashells in shimmering shades of blue and green.

"What a beautiful necklace," she said.

"It is very special," said the old woman. "I made it myself. Would you like to hear the story of why I made it?"

"Yes please," said Ella, and she sat down ready to listen as the old woman began to tell her tale.

Chapter 2

The Necklace

When I was a young girl like you, I lived here in Zennor with my father, who was a fisherman. My mother was dead, and we were very poor. Every day at low tide I would walk along the seashore collecting shells – the smaller and prettier the better.

On Sunday mornings, when the tide was high and all the good villagers were in church, I would sit on a rock in the cove and thread the shells on strings to make necklaces. Then I would sell them to the rich folk as they came out of church.

While I worked, I could hear the singing from the church. They had a fine choir, and the finest voice of all belonged to a young man called Matthew Trewella.

Matthew sang like an angel, and all the girls in the village wanted to be his sweetheart. But he never noticed them. He only wanted to sing. And I loved listening to him as I made my necklaces.

One Sunday morning, I was working as usual, threading shells on to a string, when I looked up and saw a strange lady sitting on a rock across the cove.

I had never seen her before and I was puzzled. She had not been there a moment ago and she had not walked past me. How had she got there without my seeing her? She was wearing a long sea-green cloak with a hood covering her hair, but her feet were bare. I had never seen a woman with bare feet before. The village women kept their boots on, even when they came to the cove.

When the stranger saw me looking at her, she stood up and almost danced towards me across the rocks.

"What is it you are making?" she asked, and her voice was musical and sweet. Her face was sweet too, and her eyes – well, I had never seen such eyes. Big and grey-green and shining they were, and they commanded you to look at her. I could not take my eyes off her.

"I'm making necklaces from the shells I've collected from the beach," I said. "I sell them to the rich folk when they come out of church."

The lady nodded. "They are so pretty. And tell me, please, who is singing so beautifully this morning?"

"That is Matthew Trewella," I said. "He is famous for his singing. He sings in the church on the hill every Sunday morning."

The lady nodded again. "Then I must go up to the church and listen to him properly," she said.

And with that she left me and hurried up the hill towards the church. I wanted to tell her to be careful on the stones with her bare feet, but she didn't even seem to notice them. I went on stringing my shells, thinking about the strange lady and wondering who she was.

Chapter 3

The Mermaid

Before the service ended, I saw the church door open and the lady hurry out. She ran down the hill towards the cove and climbed on to the big rock where I had first seen her. Then she turned to me and held a finger to her lips.

"If anyone asks, pray do not tell them you have seen me. Can you do that for me?" she asked.

"I shall keep it a secret."

"Thank you," she said.

And then a most strange thing happened. The lady stood up very straight and dived into the sea. And as she dived, her cloak seemed to dissolve around her and her bare feet became a glorious, shimmering fishtail.

I gasped. I had heard legends of mermaids, of course I had, but I had never thought to see one. Could this lady truly be a real live mermaid? I could hardly believe what I had seen. I longed to tell everyone about her, but I had made a promise, so I said nothing.

Even when the people hurried out of church and asked of me whether I had seen a strange lady, I shook my head. I was sure the mermaid had her reasons for not wanting to be found.

As I lay in bed that night, I recalled the stories my father had told me about mermaids, and how they were dangerous. But now I had met one, and spoken to her, and seen how beautiful and kind she was, I felt sure that my father must be wrong.

Chapter 4

The Mermaid Returns

The next Sunday I was in my usual place in the cove.

I wondered if the mermaid would come again.

Sure enough, as soon as Matthew started singing,

the mermaid appeared and sat on the rock, listening.

She wore the same long sea-green cloak with a hood,

and again her feet were bare.

She walked over to me and watched me for a moment

as I threaded my shells. "How lovely they are!" she said.

"Would you make a necklace for me?"

I looked up into her amazing grey-green eyes and nodded.

"Certainly I will," I said. "I will find the prettiest shells

I can, and when you come again next week, I will have

your necklace ready for you."

The mermaid smiled. "I am grateful to you," she said. "You are a clever girl. I will look forward to wearing it."

Then she said, "Matthew is singing again. I must go to the church and hear him."

And she walked up the hill to the church and went inside. Again she came out before the service ended, while the organ was still playing loudly, and ran down the hill towards the cove. And again she put her finger to her lips and asked me to promise not to tell that I had seen her.

"Of course," I said. "You have my word that I will keep your secret. And next week I will have your necklace ready for you."

"Thank you," she said. "You are a good child."

Then she climbed on to the rock and dived into the sea. And again as she dived, her cloak seemed to dissolve around her and her feet became a glorious, shimmering fishtail.

This time even more people came out of church and

hurried down to the cove. "Did a strange woman come

this way?" they asked, but I shook my head.

"Are you sure?" they asked, but again I shook my head.

Then Matthew himself came out of the church and down

to the cove. "Did you see the lady?" he asked me.

"The beautiful lady in the green cloak? I must find her!"

He looked so upset I was tempted to tell him,

but I remembered my promise to the mermaid.

Clearly she did not want anyone to know who she was.

Maybe she was afraid everyone would think she was

dangerous, like my father did, and be scared of her.

"No," I said. "Nobody came this way."

And Matthew walked away, looking very sad.

All that week I kept seeing him wandering down to

the cove, as if he was looking for her, though he could not

possibly know who she really was.

I was certain she had not told him herself.

While he watched and waited, I continued to search for shells, looking for the smallest and prettiest ones I could find to make into a necklace for the mermaid.

Every evening, I sorted through the shells I had collected until I had found enough to make the loveliest necklace I had ever made.

Chapter 5

The Mermaid Sings

The following Sunday I woke early, so that I could finish

the mermaid's necklace before she appeared. But some of

the shells were so tiny that it took me longer than

I had expected, and I was still working on it when I heard

the church bells ring and Matthew began to sing.

A moment later she appeared on the rock.

As she walked towards me, I called, "Forgive me, your

necklace is not yet finished. When you return from

church, it will be ready for you ... I promise."

The mermaid smiled. "It is looking beautiful already,"

she said. "I shall be pleased to wear it."

Again she hurried up the road towards the church,

and I heard the heavy door close behind her.

This time when Matthew sang, another voice joined him, and this voice was sweet and silvery. I knew instantly that it was the voice of the mermaid. They sounded wonderful singing together.

I worked fast to get her necklace finished, and I had just put the clasp on when the church door opened and the mermaid ran down the hill towards the cove. She was soon followed by Matthew himself. She looked behind her and gave a little cry as he caught up with her and took her hand.

"My darling," he cried, "Please tell me who you are!"

"No, I cannot ..." she broke off, her voice sounding choked.

"But you must stay!" Mathew declared, and sank down
on one knee. "I love you so dearly. Will you marry me?"

Again the mermaid said, "No, it cannot be!"

"But surely, you love me in return?" Matthew begged.

Tears ran down the mermaid's face as she cried,

"Of course I do. But you do not understand, I cannot
marry you. And I cannot stay here. I must leave!"

And with that, she pulled away from him and bounded
to the rock. Then she dived into the sea, and her cloak
dissolved around her and her feet turned into
a shimmering fishtail.

Matthew followed her on to the rock. He stared for
a moment at the place where she had disappeared under
the waves, then he cried, "Wait for me, my love. I will
come with you!" and jumped into the sea after her.

20

I gazed, horrified. I knew that mermaids could live underwater, but I also knew that people could not survive beneath the waves. But at the very moment that Matthew jumped, the lady rose out of the sea and caught him in her arms. They sank under the waves together.

Chapter 6

The Song of the Sea

Too late, I realised I was still holding her necklace, the one

I had made for her. She would not be wanting it now.

I put it round my own neck and packed up my shells.

When the people rushed out of church they asked me if

I had seen the lady or Matthew. And this time, because

I had made no promise to the mermaid, and because

I was worried about Matthew, I told them what I had seen.

Of course, they did not believe me. They said I was lying

and that I was very wicked, and should be ashamed of

myself for saying such things.

My father cast his net to see if he could find either

Matthew or the lady in the water, but he found nothing

and nobody.

Finally, the people went away, weeping and wailing at the loss of Matthew, leaving me with my father. I told him truly what I had seen, and he shook his head sadly.

"Ah, my daughter," he said, "I did tell you that mermaids were dangerous. Now you see why."

"But she was so beautiful, and so kind!" I protested.

Father just shook his head again. "She may have been so. But humans and sea creatures don't mix, no matter how much they may want to. No, I'm afraid poor Matthew has gone forever. Come away home, now. There is nothing more to be done."

But, later that evening, just as the sun was setting,

I went back down to the cove. I sat on my rock, holding

the lovely necklace that I had made for the mermaid and

that she would never now wear.

Then I heard something amazing. It sounded like singing –

under the waves. There were two voices: one low and

powerful, the other sweet and silvery. I knew at once

who they were. I called to my father who was mending

his nets nearby.

"Father, come and listen! They are alive – they are singing!"

He joined me in the cove and we listened. The singing

sounded even more glorious than it had in the church.

Some of the villagers came past and stopped to listen, too.

"It sounds just like Matthew," they said in astonishment.

At sunset the next evening I heard the singing again, and
this time more of the villagers came to listen.
Every evening for a while afterwards, the sweet song filled
the air, and over time the villagers came to believe
my story. They asked the rector if he would let the village
carpenter carve a mermaid in the church, in memory
of Matthew and the mermaid. The rector agreed, and
the carpenter came. I sat and watched him as he carved.
I thought his mermaid was not as beautiful as the real one,
but the villagers all loved it.

Chapter 7

The Carving

Ella had listened spellbound to the old woman. Now, when the story had finished, Ella asked eagerly, "Do they still sing under the sea? Could I hear them, do you think?" The old woman smiled. "Sometimes, at sunset, if the wind and weather are right," she said. "And only if you really want to."

"And is that the necklace you made for the mermaid?" Ella asked, pointing to the beautiful necklace round the old woman's neck.

She nodded. "And now, you must want to see the carving. It is up there, on that chair."

Ella stood up and walked towards a very old chair at the front of the church. She bent down to look.

26

Sure enough she could just make out the carving of

a mermaid. It looked very old indeed.

"It's beautiful!" she said, turning back to the old woman.

There was nobody there. Instead, just where she had been

sitting, was the shell necklace.

Ella stared at it for a moment. Where had the old woman

gone? She looked around, but there was no sign of her.

At last, Ella picked up the necklace and put it round

her neck. "The old woman must want me to have it,"

she said, just as the door opened and Dad came in.

"Did you see an old woman go out?" Ella asked.

"No," said Dad. "Nobody came past me. Why?"

Ella shook her head. "She was telling me the story

of the mermaid. And she showed me the carving on

the chair – look," and she pointed it out to Dad.

"It's really beautiful."

Dad grinned. "I thought you'd like it," he said.

"The old woman knew all about it," said Ella. "She said she saw the mermaid herself, three times, and afterwards she watched the carpenter carving her image into the chair. But she said it wasn't as beautiful as the real mermaid."

Dad laughed. "The story is very old, and this carving was done about six hundred years ago. The old woman you spoke to couldn't possibly have watched it being done."

Ella shivered. She thought about the woman's lace cap and old-fashioned clothing, and of her pale skin and bright blue eyes. Ella felt the hairs on the back of her neck prickle as she realised that the old woman she had been speaking with had actually been dead for six hundred years!

"But ... she told me the story as if she'd really been there, and I believe she really was." She broke off and touched her necklace. "And she left this for me."

"How strange," said Dad. Then he smiled. "It's a very pretty necklace, Ella. It was kind of her to give it to you."

28

"She said she'd made it for the mermaid," said Ella. "She was

here, Dad, I promise."

"Of course, if you say so," smiled Dad, and turned to leave.

Before they closed the great oak door behind them,

Ella had a last quick look round the dark, gloomy church.

Was the old woman still there somewhere in the shadows?

There was no sign of her. The last thing Ella saw as they

left was the carving of the mermaid on the chair.

"Goodbye, mermaid," she whispered, and she followed

Dad out into the sunshine.

Things to think about

1. Why do you think the girl does not tell the villagers about the mermaid until the end? Do you think she was right to keep the mermaid a secret?
2. What do you think is the most important event in the story?
3. Why don't the villagers believe the girl's story?
4. Do you think Ella's dad will believe her story about the old woman in the church?
5. Can you think of any stories related to objects or places near your home?

Write it yourself

This book tells the story of a local legend. Now try to write your own story with a similar theme. You could use a legend that already exists from your local area or invent your own. Plan your story before you begin to write it.

Start off with a story map:

• a beginning to introduce the characters and where and when your story is set (the setting);

• a problem which the main characters will need to fix in the story;

• an ending where the problems are resolved.

Get writing! Try to include geographical and historical details so that your readers get a sense of the time and place of your story, and think about the dialogue your characters would use. Would they use formal or informal language?

Notes for parents and carers

Independent reading

The aim of independent reading is to read this book with ease. This series is designed to provide an opportunity for your child to read for pleasure and enjoyment. These notes are written for you to help your child make the most of this book.

About the book

When Ella visits the church of Zennor, in Cornwall, UK, her dad tells her to look for an interesting carving. Then Ella meets a mysterious old woman who tells her all about the carving and the mermaid it depicts.

Before reading

Ask your child why they have selected this book. Look at the title and blurb together. What do they think it will be about? Do they think they will like it?

During reading

Encourage your child to read independently. If they get stuck on a longer word, remind them that they can find syllable chunks that can be sounded out from left to right. They can also read on in the sentence and think about what would make sense.

After reading

Support comprehension by talking about the story. What happened?
Then help your child think about the messages in the book that go beyond the story, using the questions on the page opposite. Give your child a chance to respond to the story, asking:
Did you enjoy the story and why? Who was your favourite character?
What was your favourite part? What did you expect to happen at the end?

Franklin Watts
First published in Great Britain in 2019
by The Watts Publishing Group

Copyright © The Watts Publishing Group 2019
All rights reserved.

Series Editors: Jackie Hamley and Melanie Palmer
Series Advisors: Dr Sue Bodman and Glen Franklin
Series Designer: Peter Scoulding

A CIP catalogue record for this book is
available from the British Library.

ISBN 978 1 4451 6527 1 (hbk)
ISBN 978 1 4451 6528 8 (pbk)
ISBN 978 1 4451 6985 9 (library ebook)

Printed in China

Franklin Watts
An imprint of
Hachette Children's Group
Part of The Watts Publishing Group
Carmelite House
50 Victoria Embankment
London EC4Y 0DZ

An Hachette UK Company
www.hachette.co.uk

www.franklinwatts.co.uk

FSC
www.fsc.org
MIX
Paper from
responsible sources
FSC® C104740